MR.  at Be

Roger Hargreaves

Original concept by
Roger Hargreaves

Written and illustrated by
Adam Hargreaves

EGMONT

There are lots of different ways to go to sleep.

Little Miss Giggles likes to giggle herself to sleep.

Little Miss Chatterbox likes to talk herself to sleep.

And Mr Tickle likes to tickle himself to sleep.

Every night, it takes Mr Greedy a very long time to go to sleep.

After cleaning his teeth, he gets into bed and then he reads his book.

Suddenly his tummy rumbles.

He is peckish.

He gets up, goes downstairs, makes himself a sandwich, eats his sandwich, goes back upstairs, brushes his teeth, again, gets into bed, again and opens his book, again.

Just as he is dropping off to sleep, his tummy rumbles.

Again!

Back downstairs, another snack, back upstairs, teeth cleaned, into bed and book opened.

Again!

And I am sure you know what happens next.

Another rumble!

So you see it takes Mr Greedy a very long time to go to sleep.

Finally, after a nine o'clock and a ten o'clock and an eleven o'clock and a midnight snack, his tummy is satisfied.

Mr Greedy has very clean teeth.

Mr Lazy on the other hand takes a very short time to go to bed.

He is already there because he never got up in the first place!

Little Miss Busy never gets to bed.

Every time she starts to climb the stairs she thinks of one last thing to do.

But it is never the last thing to do.

It is only ever the next thing to do.

All night long!

And talking of long.

Have you seen how long Mr Tall's bed is?

And how narrow Mr Skinny's bed is?

And how short Little Miss Tiny's bed is?

But Little Miss Dotty sleeps in the strangest bed.

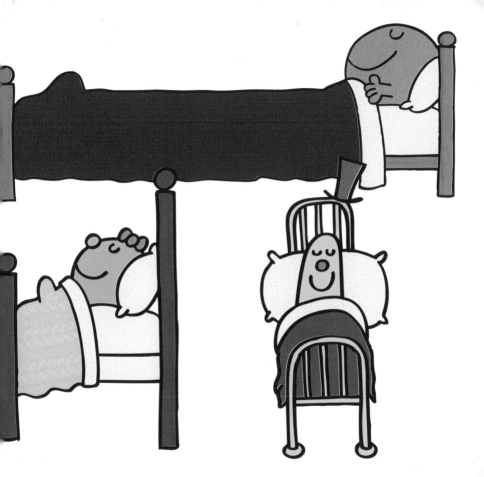

She sleeps in her flowerbed!

What a muddy bed!

Mr Silly likes a bath in jelly before bedtime.

What a sticky bath!

Of course Mr Messy does not have a bath.

He does not make his bed.

He does not even clean his teeth.

YUK!

Mr Perfect has perfectly cleaned teeth.

So clean you can see them when he turns the light out.

Mr Jelly does not turn his light out. He has a nightlight.

He is afraid of the dark.

He is also afraid of bed bugs that bite.

And things that go bump in the night.

Poor Mr Jelly.

Isn't he silly?

One thing that goes bump in the night is Mr Bump.

Falling out of bed.

BUMP!

      BUMP!

            BUMP!

All night long.

Mr Wrong on the other hand never gets into bed.

He gets into his wardrobe!

So there are lots of different ways to go to sleep.

Some of them I would not suggest you try.

But always remember one thing …

… don't have a sleepover with Mr Tickle!

It won't be bedtime, it will be tickletime!